FAXABLE
Greeting Cards

BY JOHN CALDWELL
WORKMAN PUBLISHING, NEW YORK

ACKNOWLEDGMENTS

I lovingly dedicate this book to my mother, who taught me all the right stuff and, I'm certain, would take me back should the bottom fall out of this business.

Workman Publishing Company, Inc.
708 Broadway
New York, New York 10003

Manufactured in the United States of America
First Printing March 1991
10 9 8 7 6 5 4 3 2 1

Contents

Happy Birthday

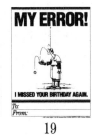
Anniversaries

Get Well Soon

I'm sorry to hear you're less than 100 percent... *...and more than 100 degrees!* GET WELL SOON.

24

I heard you're in bed with that thing that's going around. Get Well Soon.

25

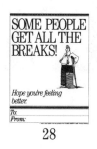

Sorry to hear you're stuck in bed. GET WELL SOON.

26

When you're not feeling up to par, you should always consult your doctor... ...it could turn out to be something simple, like a bad stance or a faulty backswing. GET WELL SOON.

27

SOME PEOPLE GET ALL THE BREAKS! *Hope you're feeling better.*

28

Invitations

REVEL WITHOUT A CAUSE! *Please attend our party!*

29

We're having a little affair at the office.

30

We're starting a rotisserie league. Care to join us?

31

ANNOUNCING OUR HOLIDAY BLOWOUT!

32

WHOOPS! I think he meant "punt." You don't have to know much about football to enjoy our Super Bowl party.

33

It's a stag party. RSVP *And you're invited!*

34

You're invited to a shower... ...and it's definitely going to pour!

35

There's a bridal shower in your forecast.

36

A shower is on the way. Be sure not to miss it.

37

COME ON OVER AND HELP US PUT AWAY THE GROCERIES. PLEASE JOIN US FOR DINNER.

38

YOU'RE INVITED TO A PARTY! PLEASE BRING:

39

WE LOVE TO ENTERTAIN

40

Thank Yous and I'm Sorrys

THIS IS JUST MY WAY OF SAYING THANK YOU.

41

THANK YOU FOR: ☐ THE LOVELY GIFT ☐ THE SPLENDID MEAL ☐ NOT SMOKING ☐

42

THANKS A HEAP!

43

I'M ONLY GOING TO SAY THIS ONCE. Thanks for letting me get it off my chest.

44

THANKS FOR PUTTING ME BACK TOGETHER.

45

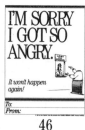

I'M SORRY I GOT SO ANGRY. *It won't happen again!*

46

I CAN'T BELIEVE I SAID THAT! **I'm sorry.**

47

Holiday Greetings

Time to wring out the old *Happy New Year!*

48

RSVP ASAP OXOXOX

49

SORRY, I JUST COULDN'T HOLD IT IN ANY LONGER!

50

I might as well face the music. You make my heart skip a beat. *Be My Valentine.*

51

You've cast a spell over me.

52

KNOWING YOU HAS BROADENED MY HORIZON. *Please stop sending me chocolates.*

53

NOW LOOK WHAT YOU'VE GONE AND DONE.

54

Today let's do something the Irish would do. Go out for a long one. Happy St. Patrick's Day
To: From:
55

ENJOY THIS EASTER... . . . take some time to bite the bunny.
To: From:
56

Break out the bubbly... ...and have a happy Mother's Day.
To: From:
57

YOU'VE TRULY MADE YOUR MARK! *Happy Mother's Day*
To: From:
58

Father's Day gives you the perfect excuse to put your feet up, down a few cold ones, and watch the tube. Tomorrow you'll have to go back to your old excuses.
To: From:
59

A toast that speaks for itself. Happy Father's Day.
To: From:
60

TAKE A LETTER! ENJOY SECRETARIES WEEK
To: From:
61

IF THE SPIRIT MOVES YOU HAVE A NICE HALLOWEEN!
To: From:
62

If I had only one wish... ...it would be that you have a wonderful Thanksgiving!
To: From:
63

A Little Holiday Cheer *YAY!*
To: From:
64

Friendship

YOU SWEPT ME OFF MY FEET... ...and filled my head with dirty thoughts.
To: From:
65

Since I fell for you... I don't know whether I'm coming or going.
To: From:
66

YOU'RE TRYING MY PATIENCE. YOU CAN FORGET ABOUT SAMPLING MY OTHER VIRTUES.
To: From:
67

When I'm not with you I get this funny feeling in the pit of my stomach. The same one I get from watching major surgery on PBS.
To: From:
68

I CAN'T IMAGINE LIFE WITHOUT YOU! Of course, I also can't imagine life without split ends.
To: From:
69

In a world that has its share of ups and downs... ...it's good to know someone who has it all together.
To: From:
70

Without your help... ...I couldn't go on.
To: From:
71

I'll come back... ...but I won't crawl.
To: From:
72

I hear you're down in the dumps. Please cheer up.
To: From:
73

GIVE ME A CALL. *MEOW!* This news can't wait.
To: From:
74

I MISS YOUR BIG SMILING FACE!
To: From:
75

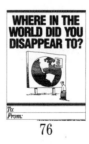
WHERE IN THE WORLD DID YOU DISAPPEAR TO?
To: From:
76

I'M AWFULLY BUSY. But for you I'll make time.
To: From:
77

The trouble with today's super-techno-sophisticated-state-of-the-art electronic society is... ...people just don't interface anymore. Give me a call so we can get together.
To: From:
78

I haven't heard from you lately. Leave a message on my machine.
To: From:
79

This is the last time I'll harp about it... ...but:
☐ You never call.
☐ You never write.
☐ You never request "Mood Indigo."
To: From:
80

Good Luck and Congratulations

IT CAN BE ROUGH OUT THERE. GOOD LUCK.	As you make your way through life's many obstacles... ...may you always leave your mark. GOOD LUCK!	FOR WHAT YOU'VE DONE... ...CONGRATULATIONS SHOULD BE IN ORDER!	Before I pat you on the back, I feel it only fair to warn you... ...I HAVE A BLACK BELT IN KUDOS!	Congratulations! I always felt you'd make your mark someday.	Congratulations on your sheepskin! Now you're dressed for success.
81	82	83	84	85	86

Special Occasions

TWO CAN LIVE AS CHEAPLY AS ONE... ...Congratulations on your marriage.	CONGRATULATIONS! I heard you took the plunge.	YOU KNOW WHAT THEY SAY ABOUT LOVE AND MARRIAGE Congratulations on your recent wedding.	I HEARD YOU TIED THE KNOT. Congratulations	ANNOUNCING THE BIRTH OF THE FIRST WOMAN PRESIDENT.	IT'S A BOY!	They'll have a hard time filling your shoes. HAPPY RETIREMENT!
87	88	89	90	91	92	93

SINCE YOU'RE FINALLY RETIRING, kick off your shoes and forget about the rat race.	SHOUT IT FROM THE ROOFTOP! Congratulations on your new home.	When I heard you bought your first home, I set out to write a poem steeped in meaning and sensitivity to commemorate this momentous occasion... BUT I COULDN'T FIND ANYTHING THAT RHYMES WITH MORTGAGE.	Have I given you my new address?	HAPPY VACATION! Hope you have a chance to unwind.
94	95	96	97	98

Have a Nice Day!

I THOUGHT MAYBE YOU COULD USE A LITTLE BOOST! HAVE A NICE DAY.	CHEER UP! Today is the first day of the rest of the week.	Don't let the clowns bring you down. Have a great day!
99	100	101

BEFORE YOU DO ANYTHING ELSE, HAVE A HAPPY BIRTHDAY!

To:

From:

Faxable
Greeting
Card
#1

HAPPY BIRTHDAY

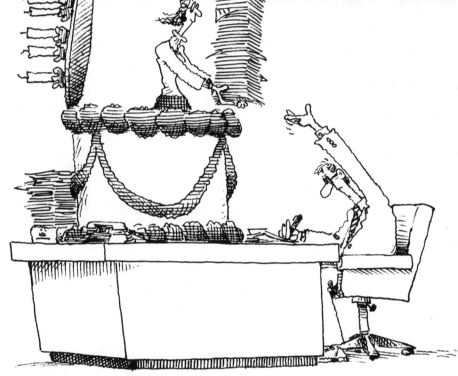

TO A REAL TYPE A!

To:

From:

IT WAS ON THE TIP OF MY TONGUE

HAPPY BIRTHDAY!

BUT IT MOVED TO THE TOP OF MY LUNGS.

To:

From:

It's your birthday...

BOB'S NUDIST CAMP

...drop everything and celebrate!

To:

From:

WHAT'S WRONG WITH THIS PICTURE?

1. By the dog's foggy expression, it's plain to see he doesn't know what day it is. I do.

2. It's obvious that the guy in the suit isn't going to bend over backwards to send you a birthday card. Thank goodness for friends like me.

3. No matter how many legs she has to stand on, this woman has no excuse for forgetting your birthday. And neither do I.

HAPPY BIRTHDAY!

To:

From:

YOU'RE ONLY AS OLD AS YOU FEEL.

CAUTION: **SOME PARTS FEEL OLDER THAN OTHERS.**

HAPPY BIRTHDAY!

To:

From:

I REMEMBERED YOUR BIRTHDAY.

The least you can do is forget your diet.

To:

From:

Faxable
Greeting
Card
#7

What has two arms, two legs, and forty candles?

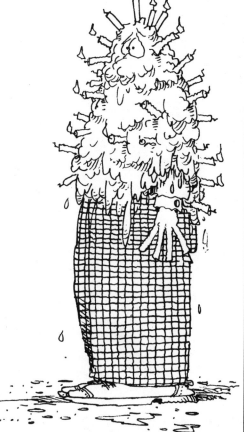

HAPPY BIRTHDAY.

To:

From:

Hey!
It's your birthday.

Loosen your tie
and let down
your hair.

To:

From:

HAPPY BIRTHDAY!

Bet you thought I'd forget.

To:

From:

I just discovered what day this is...

HAPPY BIRTHDAY.

To:

From:

Faxable
Greeting
Card
#11

HAS ANYONE EVER TOLD YOU YOU'RE GORGEOUS?

Well... then... has anyone ever told you to have a nice birthday?

To:

From:

You've reached that awkward age. Your liver spots outnumber your hickeys.

HAPPY BIRTHDAY

To:

From:

I'M SO ASHAMED.

It's not like me to forget your birthday.

To:

From:

I MISSED THE BOAT

Belated Birthday Wishes

To:

From:

SORRY I MISSED YOUR BIRTHDAY.

I just caught wind of it. Many Happy Returns.

To:

From:

BELATED WISHES

HOLY MOSES!
I FORGOT YOUR BIRTHDAY.

To:

From:

SORRY I MISSED YOUR BIRTHDAY.

I got tied up.

To:

From:

MY ERROR!

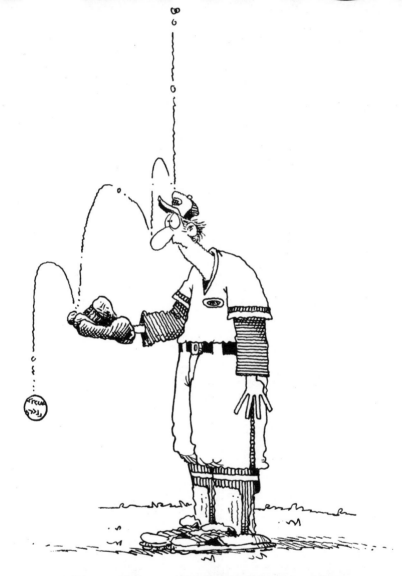

I MISSED YOUR BIRTHDAY AGAIN.

To:

From:

THUMBS UP!

To: _____

From: _____

I've been keeping track.

HAPPY ANNIVERSARY!

To:

From:

The fun is just beginning!

Happy Anniversary.

To:

From:

Your anniversary is definitely something to howl about.

OWOOOOOO!

Pardon my laryngitis.

To:

From:

A FAXABLE GREETING

I'm sorry to hear you're less than 100 percent...

...and more than 100 degrees!

GET WELL SOON.

To:

From:

I heard you're in bed with that thing that's going around.

Get Well Soon.

To:

From:

Sorry to hear you're stuck in bed.

GET WELL SOON.

To:

From:

When you're not feeling up to par, you should always consult your doctor . . .

. . . it could turn out to be something simple, like a bad stance or a faulty backswing.

GET WELL SOON.

To:

From:

SOME PEOPLE GET ALL THE BREAKS!

Hope you're feeling better.

To:

From:

REVEL WITHOUT A CAUSE!

Please attend our party!

Date: _____

Time: _____

Place: _____

RSVP: _____

To: _____

From: _____

We're having a little affair at the office.

Date:

Time:

Place:

RSVP:

To:

From:

We're starting a rotisserie league.

Care to join us?

To:

From:

ANNOUNCING OUR HOLIDAY BLOWOUT!

DATE:_____

TIME:_____

PLACE:_____

RSVP:_____

To:

From:

WHOOPS!

I think he meant "punt."

You don't have to know much about football to enjoy our Super Bowl party.

DATE: _____   PLACE: _____

TIME: _____   RSVP: _____

To:

From:

It's a stag party.

And you're invited!

Date: _____   Place: _____

Time: _____   RSVP: _____

To:

From:

You're invited to a shower . . .

. . . and it's definitely going to pour!

Date: _____
Time: _____
Place: _____
RSVP: _____

To:

From:

There's a bridal shower in your forecast.

Date:
Time:
Place:
RSVP:

To:

From:

A shower is on the way.

Be sure not to miss it.

Date: _____   Place: _____

Time: _____   RSVP: _____

To:

From:

COME ON OVER AND HELP US PUT AWAY THE GROCERIES.

PLEASE JOIN US FOR DINNER.

DATE:

TIME:

PLACE:

RSVP:

To:

From:

YOU'RE INVITED TO A PARTY!

PLEASE BRING:

☐ **A guest of your choice.**

☐ **A guest of my choice.**

☐ **All the Elvis impersonators you can scrape up on short notice.**

DATE:_____

TIME:_____

PLACE:_____

RSVP:_____

*To:*_____

*From:*_____

WE LOVE TO ENTERTAIN

☐ **So come on over for dinner and drinks.**

☐ **Stop by for brunch and banjo music.**

☐ **Drop in for tasty victuals and our virtuoso, soul-stirring 30-song tribute to the legendary music of Trini Lopez.**

DATE:

PLACE:

TIME:

RSVP:

To:

From:

THIS IS JUST MY WAY OF SAYING THANK YOU.

To:

From:

THANK YOU FOR:

- ☐ **THE LOVELY GIFT**
- ☐ **THE SPLENDID MEAL**
- ☐ **NOT SMOKING**
- ☐ _____

To:

From:

THANKS A HEAP!

To:

From:

I'M ONLY GOING TO SAY THIS ONCE.

THIS ONCE.

Thanks for letting me get it off my chest.

To:

From:

THANKS FOR PUTTING ME BACK TOGETHER.

To:

From:

I'M SORRY I GOT SO ANGRY.

It won't happen again!

To:

From:

I CAN'T BELIEVE I SAID THAT!

I'm sorry.

To:

From:

Time to wring out the old.

Happy New Year!

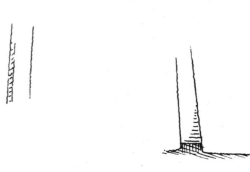

To:

From:

RSVP
ASAP

OXOXOX

To:

From:

Faxable
Greeting
Card
#49

SORRY, I JUST COULDN'T HOLD IT IN ANY LONGER!

To:

From:

I might as well face the music.

You make my heart skip a beat.

Be My Valentine.

To:

From:

You've cast a spell over me.

LUHV

To:

From:

Faxable
Greeting
Card
#52

KNOWING YOU HAS BROADENED MY HORIZON.

Please stop sending me chocolates.

To:

From:

NOW LOOK WHAT YOU'VE GONE AND DONE.

To:

From:

Today let's do something the Irish would do.

Go out for a long one.

Happy St. Patrick's Day

To:

From:

Faxable
Greeting
Card
#55

ENJOY THIS EASTER...

... take some time to bite the bunny.

To:

From:

Break out the bubbly...

...and have a happy Mother's Day.

To:

From:

YOU'VE TRULY MADE YOUR MARK!

Happy Mother's Day

To:

From:

Father's Day gives you the perfect excuse to put your feet up, down a few cold ones, and watch the tube.

Tomorrow you'll have to go back to your old excuses.

To:

From:

Faxable
Greeting
Card
#59

A toast that speaks for itself.

Happy Father's Day.

To:

From:

TAKE A LETTER!

ENJOY SECRETARIES WEEK

To:

From:

IF THE SPIRIT MOVES YOU

HAVE A NICE HALLOWEEN!

To:

From:

If I had only one wish...

...it would be that you have a wonderful Thanksgiving!

To:

From:

A Little Holiday Cheer

HO HO HO

YAY!

To:

From:

YOU SWEPT ME OFF MY FEET...

...and filled my head with dirty thoughts.

To:

From:

Since I fell for you...

I don't know whether I'm coming or going.

To:

From:

YOU'RE TRYING MY PATIENCE.

YOU CAN FORGET ABOUT SAMPLING MY OTHER VIRTUES.

To:

From:

When I'm not with you I get this funny feeling in the pit of my stomach.

The same one I get from watching major surgery on PBS.

To:

From:

Faxable
Greeting
Card
#68

I CAN'T IMAGINE LIFE WITHOUT YOU!

Of course, I also can't imagine life without split ends.

To:

From:

In a world that has its share of ups and downs...

...it's good to know someone who has it all together.

To:

From:

Faxable
Greeting
Card
#70

Without your help . . .

. . . I couldn't go on.

To:

From:

I'll come back...

...but I won't crawl.

To:

From:

Faxable
Greeting
Card
#72

I hear you're down in the dumps.

Please cheer up.

To:

From:

GIVE ME A CALL.

This news can't wait.

To:

From:

I MISS YOUR BIG SMILING FACE!

To:

From:

WHERE IN THE WORLD DID YOU DISAPPEAR TO?

To:

From:

I'M AWFULLY BUSY.

But for you I'll make time.

To:

From:

The trouble with today's super-techno-sophisticated-state-of-the-art electronic society is . . .

. . . people just don't interface anymore.

Give me a call so we can get together.

To:

From:

I haven't heard from you lately.

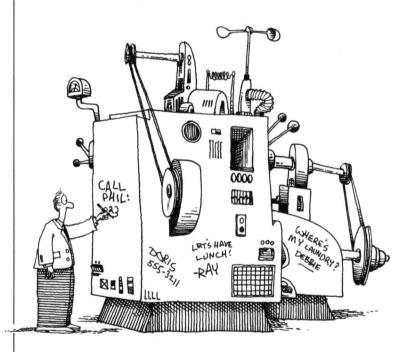

Leave a message on my machine.

To:

From:

This is the last time I'll harp about it...

...but:

☐ You never call.
☐ You never write.
☐ You never request "Mood Indigo."

To:

From:

IT CAN BE ROUGH OUT THERE.

GOOD LUCK.

To:

From:

As you make your way through life's many obstacles...

...may you always leave your mark.

GOOD LUCK!

To:

From:

FOR WHAT YOU'VE DONE...

...CONGRATULATIONS SHOULD BE IN ORDER!

To:

From:

Before I pat you on the back, I feel it only fair to warn you . . .

. . . I HAVE A BLACK BELT IN KUDOS!

To:

From:

Congratulations!

I always felt you'd make your mark someday.

To:

From:

Faxable
Greeting
Card
#85

Congratulations on your sheepskin.

Now you're dressed for success.

To:

From:

TWO CAN LIVE AS CHEAPLY AS ONE...

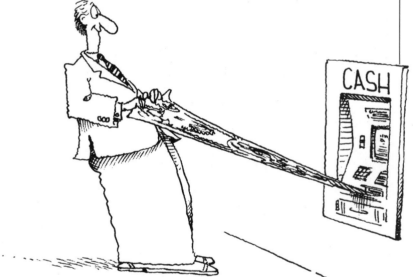

...Congratulations on your marriage.

To:

From:

CONGRATULATIONS!

*I heard
you took the plunge.*

To:

From:

YOU KNOW WHAT THEY SAY ABOUT LOVE AND MARRIAGE

Congratulations on your recent wedding.

To:

From:

I HEARD YOU TIED THE KNOT.

Congratulations

To:

From:

Faxable
Greeting
Card
#90

ANNOUNCING THE BIRTH OF THE FIRST WOMAN PRESIDENT.

To:

From:

IT'S A BOY!

COLOR KEY
1. BLUE
2. RED
3. BROWN
4. GREEN

To:

From:

They'll have a hard time filling your shoes.

HAPPY RETIREMENT!

To:

From:

SINCE YOU'RE FINALLY RETIRING,

kick off your shoes and forget about the rat race.

To:

From:

A FAXABLE GREETING

SHOUT IT FROM THE ROOFTOP!

Congratulations on your new home.

To:

From:

When I heard you bought your first home, I set out to write a poem steeped in meaning and sensitivity to commemorate this momentous occasion . . .

BUT I COULDN'T FIND ANYTHING THAT RHYMES WITH MORTGAGE.

To:

From:

Have I given you my new address?

To:

From:

HAPPY VACATION!

Hope you have a chance to unwind.

To:

From:

I THOUGHT MAYBE YOU COULD USE A LITTLE BOOST!

HAVE A
NICE DAY.

To:

From:

CHEER UP!

Today is the first day of the rest of the week.

To:

From:

Don't let the clowns bring you down.

Have a great day!

To:

From:

Faxable
Greeting
Card
#101